This Walker book belongs to:

_____

_____

_____

For Luke

First published 1998 by Walker Books Ltd
87 Vauxhall Walk, London SE11 5HJ

This edition published 2014

2 4 6 8 10 9 7 5 3 1

© 1998 Piers Harper

The right of Piers Harper to be identified as author/illustrator
of this work has been asserted by him in accordance with
the Copyright, Designs and Patents Act 1988

This book has been typeset in Maiandra

Printed in China

British Library Cataloguing in Publication Data:
a catalogue record for this book is available from the British Library

ISBN 978-0-7445-6331-3

www.walker.co.uk

If You Love a Bear

Piers Harper

WALKER BOOKS
AND SUBSIDIARIES
LONDON · BOSTON · SYDNEY · AUCKLAND

If you love a bear
you will know that bears
like to be woken up gently.

Then they jump out of bed
and run to the kitchen to make breakfast.

Bears eat a lot more than children do.

If you love a bear
you will know that bears don't wear clothes.

They don't know where to put them.

Instead they run races ...

and dance dances.

If you love a bear
you will know that bears like being outside.

They find interesting things ...

and play peek-a-boo.

Sometimes bears get cross.
They stamp about
and shout.

It's not easy loving bears
when they're like that.

A good thing to do
is to give them a small snack.
Being cross makes bears hungry.

If you love a bear
you will know that bears like having baths.
They make big bear waves.

And when they get out they like to be tickled.
It makes them wriggle and
giggle and jiggle.

If you love a bear
you will know that bears
like to go to bed when
they're sleepy.

They yawn big yawns.

Then they snuggle you up in a soft cosy
blanket and give you bear hugs.

Everyone should have a bear to love.

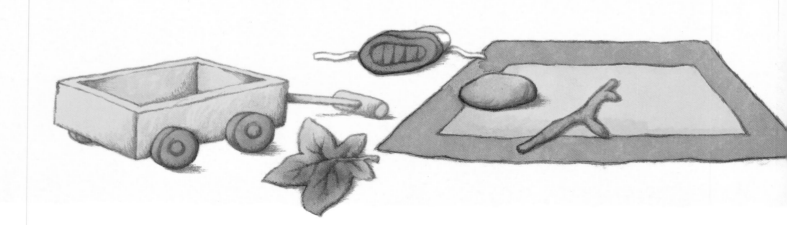